Out in the Country

Judy Pedersen

ALFRED A. KNOPF · NEW YORK

This is a Borzoi Book Published by Alfred A. Knopf, Inc.

Copyright © 1991 by Judy Pedersen
All rights reserved under International and Pan-American Copyright
Conventions. Published in the United States by Alfred A. Knopf, Inc.,
New York, and simultaneously in Canada by Random House of Canada
Limited, Toronto. Distributed by Random House, Inc., New York.
Manufactured in Singapore
Book design by Elizabeth Hardie

2   4   6   8   10   9   7   5   3   1

Library of Congress Cataloging-in-Publication Data
Pedersen, Judy. Out in the country / by Judy Pedersen.
p.   cm.
Summary: A family moves to a beautiful place in the country
and builds a new house to start their new life.
ISBN 0-679-80630-X (trade)
ISBN 0-679-90630-4 (lib. bdg.)
[1. Building—Fiction.   2. Dwellings—Fiction.
3. Country life—Fiction.]   I. Title. PZ7.P34240u   1991
[E]—dc20   90-40032   CIP   AC

The illustrations for this book were done in
wet and dry pastel on pastel cloth.

For my grandparents,
Helen and Martin,
who gave us the land

When I was very small,
we moved
from our Brooklyn apartment
to a quiet little
New England town.

My grandparents had given us land.
"Get out of the city," they'd said,
"and build yourselves a house in the country."
And that's just what we decided to do.

At first
we lived in a makeshift cabin
on a large pond.

A sappy peach tree
grew alongside the pond.
When the warm, fuzzy peaches
were ripe,
my grandmother and I
made peach preserves.

Willowy, silver birches
and wild blackberry bushes
grew in our backyard, and

a cool, clear creek
followed the edge of our yard
to a beaver dam,
then tumbled over
into another pond
and the deep woods.

One morning,
as the sun rose above the trees,
we began the work
on our new house.

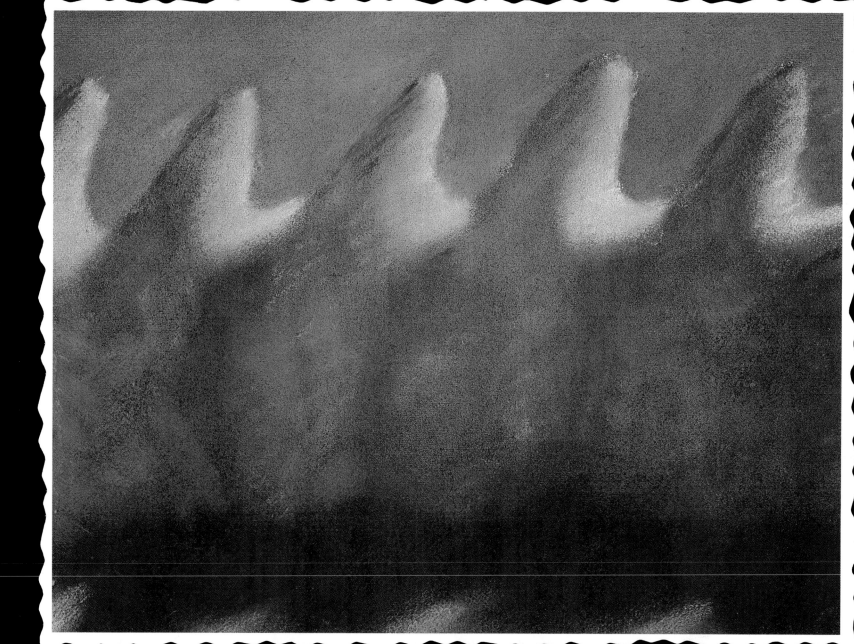

Between a tall black locust
and a spindly white ash,
my father drove a long pine stake
into the ground.

I was the north corner,
and my brother was the south.
One by one,
we measured the corners of our house
in the grass.

"Building a house takes a long time,"
my mother told us,
"and we'll need help."
My uncles piled rocks—
flat, round, and squarish—
in rows
to make a foundation.

The men framed our house
with long planks
of good-smelling spruce.
And when they were finished,
we could see the clouds and stars
through the openings.

Bit by bit,
they began to close the house in
with walls.
A bricklayer
built a chimney
and then we had a large
open
fireplace.

Before long,
our house needed a roof.
Hundreds and hundreds
of little cedar shingles
wove our house a hat.

And in the autumn,
at the end of a long
sunny day,
when the days had become shorter
and the nights had become longer,
our house was finally finished.

Judy Pedersen

grew up out in the country, in Rhinebeck, New York, and has drawn upon memory and experience to make this book. She is the author and illustrator of *The Tiny Patient* and the illustrator of *The Yellow Button* by Anne Mazer. She now lives in New York City and teaches painting at the School of Visual Arts.

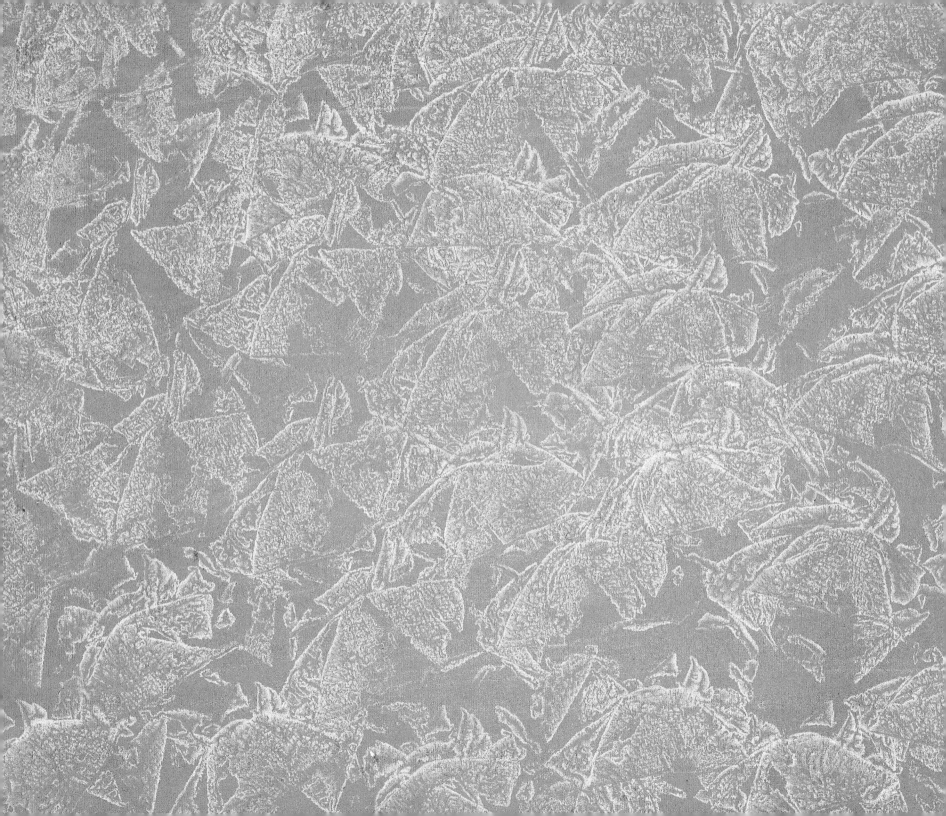